Meet Martha

Written by Karen Barss

Based on the characters created by Susan Meddaugh

HOUGHTON MIFFLIN HARCOURT

Boston • New York • 2010

Martha Speaks
Picture Clue Key

alphabet soup

letters

burger

Martha

bus

paint

family

pizza

flower

telephone

Helen

garden

WGBH

Copyright © 2010 WGBH Educational Foundation and Susan Meddaugh. "MARTHA" and all characters and underlying materials (including artwork) from the "MARTHA" books are copyright, trademarks, and registered trademarks of Susan Meddaugh and used under license. All other characters and underlying materials are trademarks of and copyright of WGBH. All rights reserved. The PBS KIDS logo is a registered mark of PBS and is used with permission.

For information about permission to reproduce selections from this book, write to Permissions, Houghton Mifflin Harcourt Publishing Company, 215 Park Avenue South, New York, New York 10003.

Library of Congress Cataloging-in-Publication Data is on file.

ISBN 978-0-547-36904-4

Design by Bill Smith Group.

www.hmhbooks.com
www.marthathetalkingdog.com

Manufactured in China / LEO 10 9 8 7 6 5 4 3 2
4500252500

Meet Martha.

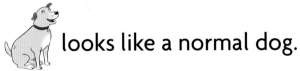 looks like a normal dog.

She likes to dig in the .

And she likes to dig in the trash!

 likes to be petted and scratched.

She loves to eat.

Did you know can order a ?

Yes,  is one special dog.

She can talk!

How is that possible?

One day  ate  .

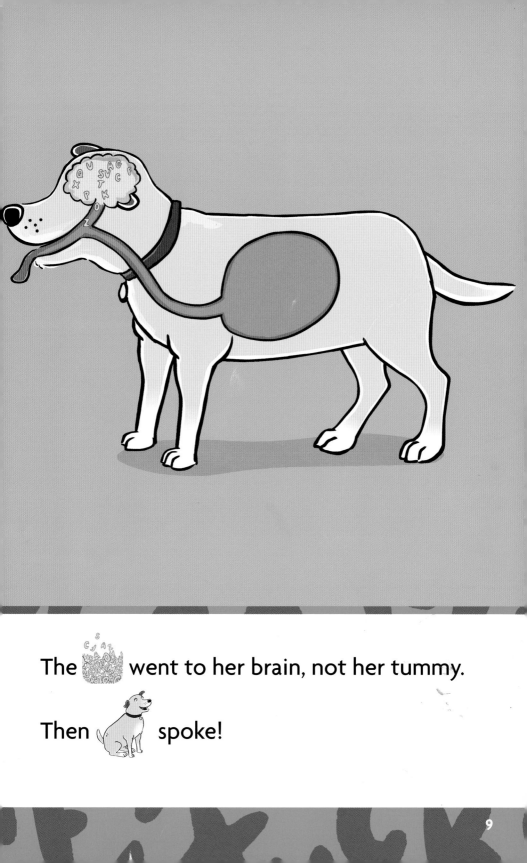

The went to her brain, not her tummy.

Then spoke!

Martha's 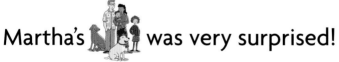 was very surprised!

 told them all about her life.

Finally, she could tell them what she was thinking!

and are best friends.

 likes to draw and ✎.

🐕 gives 🧍 advice.

Helen's mom works in a  shop.

Sometimes  helps out.

Helen's dad drives a .

 chats and keeps him company.

Helen's little brother is Jake.

 is helping him learn to speak.

Martha's brother is Skits, who does not talk.

So  tells the what his barks mean.

But sometimes  talks too much!

She ordered  on the  . . .

then her  found out!

Sometimes  surprises people.

Words can be fun.
Words can also be very useful.

Words helped when was in the dog shelter without her collar.

And one time,  even stopped a burglar!

Her  was very proud.

 is one lucky dog. She can speak!

And her family loves her very much.

Don't miss these
MARTHA SPEAKS
adventures:

MARTHA SPEAKS
Shelter Dog Blues
Based on the characters created by SUSAN MEDDAUGH

MARTHA SPEAKS
Martha on the Case
WANTED
2 Crime Stories
Based on the characters created by SUSAN MEDDAUGH

MARTHA SPEAKS
A Pup's Tale
Based on the characters created by SUSAN MEDDAUGH

Chapter books

LEVEL 2 MARTHA SPEAKS
A Picture Reader
Meet Martha
Hi there!
Based on the characters created by SUSAN MEDDAUGH

LEVEL 2 MARTHA SPEAKS
Farm Dog Martha
Based on the characters created by SUSAN MEDDAUGH

LEVEL 2 MARTHA SPEAKS
Play Ball!
Based on the characters created by SUSAN MEDDAUGH

LEVEL 2 MARTHA SPEAKS
Toy Trouble
Based on the characters created by SUSAN MEDDAUGH

Early readers

MARTHA SPEAKS
Martha Says It with Flowers
Based on the characters created by SUSAN MEDDAUGH

MARTHA SPEAKS
Leader of the Pack
Based on the characters created by SUSAN MEDDAUGH

Picture books